THE

DRAGON

IN MY WARDROBE

Copyright © 2022 by William Lusted

All rights reserved.

No part of this publication may be reproduced, distributed, or transmitted
in any form or by any means, including photocopying, recording, or other
electronic or mechanical methods, without the prior written permission of
the publisher, except as permitted by UK copyright law.

The story, all names, characters, and incidents portrayed in this production
are fictitious. No identification with actual persons (living or deceased), places,
buildings, and products is intended or should be inferred.

Book Cover & Illustrations by William Lusted.

This (second) edition published in 2023.

"An exciting tale of a young Thomas Jones and his adventure in finding a dragon.

Who should he tell, who can he trust? With an inquisitive best friend named Olive and Dad in the pest control business, facing the responsibility of this discovery is not straightforward; the pros and cons, what does it like to eat, will it burn the house down?

The more Thomas learns, the more he discovers his desire for his newfound friend to have the best life possible, even if it means sacrificing his (and Olive's) own happiness."

Joanne Woolgar, Maidstone Library, Kent, UK

CHAPTER 1

I sat in my room, reading a book at night (teehee - Mum will never find out). It was about Vikings, and how they slayed dragons. If I were them, I thought to myself, I'd side with the dragons.

Anyway, I heard a noise after that, almost like a growl, or a snarl. I looked up, stared at the room for a moment, shrugged and went back to the book. But soon after… another growl: this time louder. I looked around again, confused, but for the rest of the night I never heard another sound.

The next day at school, I told my best friend, Olive, about the strange noises I heard. You can trust her with anything, but even she struggled for an answer and then said, "Must have been your ears playing tricks on you."

The next night I was deep in my book, when I thought I heard some scratching noises, then a growl. Was it my ears playing tricks again? I doubt that. I listened carefully and noted where the noises were coming from. The wardrobe was my final answer. So I opened it up and… out leaped a killer clown head, blood covering its face!

I leapt back in terror, heart pounding, but after looking at it more, I realised it was just a costume mask from last year's Halloween. But when I looked back up at the wardrobe, I saw what looked like a tiny lizard resting on some old clothes. Were those wings on it's back? It was probably just an old toy; maybe from when I was younger. To be honest, I couldn't really tell at first in the dim light of the moon.

Hang on, did it just blink at me? Must be my mind playing tricks on me. Maybe the double maths lesson today had an effect on me.

I leaned forward, inspecting it closer, and then jumped back in surprise, as its tail flicked my face. I rubbed my eyes, is this a dream? Then, suddenly, it sped across the floor and raced underneath my bed. I looked down, but it must have been hiding as I couldn't see anything at all. Though to be honest, with the amount of mess under my bed I probably couldn't have spotted a fully grown elephant under there!

After what felt like hours of searching under my bed, I still couldn't find it. Did this thing even exist? Probably not, besides I was too tired to bother with it now.

But as much as I tried I just couldn't sleep. The further it went into the night, and the more I tossed and turned, the more I thought about that thing, its vivid red scales and what looked like wings. One word repeated in my mind: DRAGON.

Eventually, I fell asleep, dreaming and wondering...

The next morning, I woke up, rubbed my eyes and looked around the room, thinking to myself "What a strange dream." The clock showed 6:55 and it was still early morning, so I layed in bed thinking about the day ahead. My mind kept coming back to the events of the night before… The more I thought about it, the stranger it sounded.

I got up to open my curtains. The sunshine blasted into my eyes, illuminating the room. I looked back at my wardrobe and noticed the door was slightly open. Must be just a coincidence, it can't be related to last night. Can it?

I opened the wardrobe door and stood there frozen for a second, then my reflexes kicked in and I jumped back… it was instantly recognisable, what with vivid red scales, small wings tucked into its body and a sharp pointed tail.

I could see small sparks erupt from it's nostrils every time it breathed out. I took small steps towards it then I felt something below my foot, I looked down. Scorch marks. Suddenly getting close up to this thing didn't seem like such a good idea. If this thing could burn carpet, goodness knows what it could do to me.

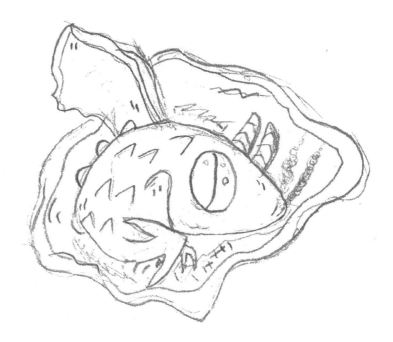

I thought about it a little more, and came up with the pros and cons of owning a dragon:

Pros:
- I would have the coolest pet in school (even if I couldn't tell anyone about it)
- It would make a great bodyguard

- It would be a good source of warmth

Cons:
- Would freak out the whole town if seen
- Could run off without warning
- Possibility of burning the house down

After thinking about the cons, I realised that having a pet dragon isn't as glamorous as it sounds.

"Thomas, time for breakfast!" Mum called up the stairs. "One more minute, Mum!" I called down... then the dragon suddenly perked up its head and looked around.

"Thomas David Jones, get down stairs right now or we'll be late for school!" I searched my head for any excuse not to go to school today... I can't leave this creature unattended, who knows what will happen to it, or if I'll ever see it again? I finally came up with a pathetic excuse and shouted back downstairs "I feel sick..." but Mum clearly wasn't buying it. "And even if you were sick you'd have to work in your room." I didn't want that. Trust me, home school is horrible. Sigh. I have a whole agonising school day ahead of me...

And with that, I picked up a few cuddly toys and used them to hide the dragon, and headed to school.

When I got to school I told Olive about the scorch marks and she said 'This thing might actually be...a dragon! Wow.'. She obviously wanted one too. But I didn't know where my "dragon" came from or even if it was a dragon at all. So there was no way I could think of to get Olive one...

CHAPTER 2

Finding Olive a dragon would have to wait, I guess. I needed to train mine. I walked up to it, avoiding the scorch mark this time. I held my hand out and braced myself, but a few seconds later I felt a tiny cold push on my hand. It was the dragon. I tried not to get too excited, but it easily got the better of me.

A few hours later I was called down for dinner. As I walked down the stairs an idea hit me. This could be the perfect opportunity to see what my dragon eats! But I'm not sure if I want to know what it's been eating already…

I ate as quickly as possible and couldn't wait to get back up to my room, I was going to sneak up some broccoli, fish fingers and fries (with ketchup, of course; everything tastes better with ketchup). I had a knight costume in my room, so I could use the shield to protect me in case the dragon tries to burn my head off. But before I could leave, Mum asked why I kept disappearing up to my room all of a sudden… I squirmed a little, then came out with a random excuse, "I found a new toy under my bed…" A few seconds passed, that felt like ages, before she replied "Well, okay then." and she walked upstairs with the washing. "Phew…" I thought, but I was getting distracted.

I raced up the stairs and opened my bedroom door, and I saw the dragon resting on the floor. But when I shut the door, it woke up and hopped onto my bed. "Now the testing can begin…" I thought.

I breathed a sigh of relief at finally being alone with my dragon, and walked towards the bed. I pulled the piece of broccoli out of my pocket, but the dragon immediately turned its nose up at it. He ate the fish, but didn't seem too keen on that either (I didn't know if it was a he or a she but I couldn't keep saying 'it'). When I pulled the fries out, though, he leapt onto my hand and guzzled them down, biting my finger in the process. As I rubbed my finger, he went back onto the bed and gave me a look that seemed to say, "Got any more?" I smiled, and it soon grew into a wide grin.

So I know what my dragon eats; that's a plus. But it won't be long before Mum catches on, especially when she sees the scorch mark… I talked about it with Olive on my phone but she just wanted to talk about getting her own dragon.

After school the next day I thought there wasn't really much to do; but when I remembered the dragon, I realised there was a LOT to do. There was only one thing I *really* wanted to do when I got home - name my dragon.

On the way home from school I had been thinking about names. I thought about Scorch or Frazzle but remembered how small it was and they didn't seem to fit. I came up with Sparky or Scales but they didn't work either… By the time I got home I started thinking about what I was going to give him to eat and then I remembered he loves fries… and what goes with fries? Ketchup….The perfect name! But when I went into my room I saw something I never wanted to see…

Or rather, some*one*…

CHAPTER 3

No no no no no no. MUM. "Er… Errmmm…"
I spluttered. Mum had her arms crossed and was
standing by the scorch mark.

"Oh no" I muttered.

"What's this?" she demanded, pointing at the scorch
mark.

"Errmmm…" I said, still speechless. I looked around
and spotted a remote control car. "Er…My…Ermm..
Car's batteries…..Exploded?"I gave a sheepish smile.
Mum's eyes narrowed. "Why on earth didn't you let me
know? About a FIRE?!"

I could see she was getting angry. "Er…Yes? I mean,
sorry?" I said, not really sure of the right answer as I was

too busy trying to see where the dragon had got to.

Mum sighed and I could see she had calmed down a bit. But just then I saw a scaly tail coming out of the wardrobe. The dragon jumped onto my bed and hid under the covers. Mum peered over and asked 'What was that?!' Then an idea popped into my head: 'It's the new toy!' I exclaimed. 'The one I was telling you about.' I picked up the dragon and showed Mum.

"Are those… sequins?"

I could feel the dragon getting irritated as Mum moved the 'sequins' revealing his vulnerable pink flesh beneath. 'Hang in there little buddy…' I thought as Mum smiled and said "Well let's get this mark cleaned up, it shouldn't be much harder than a stain". Then finally she left the room to get the cleaning stuff. I thought to myself "Phew! That was close…"

I went back downstairs to offer to help Mum clean up the scorch mark. By the time we had finished it was late. I got ready for bed and snuggled under the covers. It turned out my theory about the night light was right! It was warm and cosy under the covers, and well-lit too! As I eventually drifted off to sleep I whispered to Ketchup, 'I love having a dragon…'

When I woke up the following morning I realised it was the weekend - perfect! Now I had 2 full days to study Ketchup some more. But as I stretched under the covers I heard Mum calling me to come downstairs. Once I had finished breakfast I sped back to my room. I couldn't see Ketchup anywhere and for a moment my stomach flipped and I thought I'd lost him. But then I saw a scaly tail poking out from the covers. 'Phew' I breathed but couldn't fully relax yet: Mum was getting really suspicious after the 'incident'…

After another warm and cozy sleep with Ketchup I soon
realised Olive was coming over after school tomorrow.
I didn't mind as long as I still had time to study. I went
upstairs and gave Ketchup some fries I had snuck up.
While Ketchup ate his breakfast I took some pictures
on my phone, just in case he wouldn't come out when
Olive came. I even printed out the best one, he looked
so sweet! I smiled and picked up Ketchup and looked
after and studied him for the rest of the day.

The next day at school Olive was pumped at seeing Ketchup for the first time. She wouldn't stop talking about him for the whole day. Or asking questions for that matter; 'How big is he?' 'Tiny', 'Can he fly?' 'I don't know', 'Does he breathe fire?' 'Just sparks so far'. It carried on like that until it was finally home time.

But that didn't mean the end of the questions, oh no. She walked home with me asking even more, most of which I answered in groans. When we got home, Olive raced upstairs not even stopping to take her coat off, clearly excited to see Ketchup. Honestly, I don't blame her. After all it's not every day that you get to see a real live mythical creature. I ran up after her, but she was obviously at full speed and when she got up to my room...

"OH. MY. GOSH!!" That's all Olive could say after seeing the tiny creature resting on the bed. The noise woke him up, but instead of hiding he shot a few sparks in the air. That only made Olive even more excited, and by the smug look on his face I could tell he was enjoying the spotlight. "So do you like him?" I asked. I waited but got no response. Olive was just as astounded as I was when I first saw him. Ketchup, lapping up the attention, jumped onto Olive's shoulder. I could hear her whisper 'Wow'. What was now everyday to me must have been really exciting for Olive. She was completely speechless. She seemed excited, shocked and astonished all at the same time.

I could see Olive *loved* Ketchup, but I doubt he enjoyed anything but the attention. A bit selfish, I guess. But that didn't matter. Olive and I loved the visit and now I have someone else who knows about Ketchup. It felt good. Keeping it a secret for so long just drained me.

CHAPTER 4

After meeting my dragon Olive still asked questions, in fact I think she was asking even more; I didn't mind though. As long as I could let it out, it felt so great to have told someone. Mum said she wanted me to get some 'fresh air' with her, and I soon realised that leaving Ketchup at home was probably the best idea. But even that could go wrong, what with Dad staying at home. He's part of pest control so goodness knows what he might do if he found Ketchup. But that was my only option. I just hoped Mum wouldn't notice the panicked expression on my face. She did. 'Are you alright?' she asked as we walked down the driveway. I had no answer. 'Is something wrong?'

'No Mum.' I answered reluctantly.

But, being my Mum, she had learnt that 'no' actually meant 'yes'. 'Come on love, you can tell me.'

But of course I couldn't tell her, because:

1. She wouldn't believe me anyway and
2. Because I couldn't risk another person knowing, even if she is my Mum.

So in the end I had to come up with another excuse. "Errr…" I mumbled, "I lost my toy, the sequined one." "Well, that's a shame." Mum said. But then she smiled and asked "Where did you get yours from? We can get a new one online."

"No" I said.

"Surely we can find you a new one" Mum said, taking out her phone.

"N-No." I stammered, "They're..err…out of stock!"

"Oh…"Mum answered, looking a little hurt.

"Never mind." I said, breaking the silence. "I'm sure I

can find it."

Mum smiled at this and I breathed a sigh of relief, phew!

When I got home I could tell Dad hadn't found Ketchup, so far so good. I went upstairs and ran into my room and saw Ketchup on the bed with an expectant look on his face. "Sorry buddy" I said and he looked disappointed that I didn't give him any fries. He slumped forward onto the bed. I then heard a faint whirring noise - the whirring of a vacuum cleaner. I opened my door and saw Dad outside, vacuuming. "Hi Dad." I said.

"Hi," he replied. He then walked into my room and started vacuuming "No! Wait!" I shouted over the noise of the vacuum cleaner, Dad turned and looked at me blankly.

"My toy, the dragon one. I lost it, and you might... err... vacuum it up!" I rambled.

"Ah yes, your Mother told me about that." Then he
smiled and said, "I guess it can't hurt to leave one room
for now," and with that he went back downstairs.

Once Dad had gone, I breathed a sigh of relief. "You
can come out now." I said, and smiled as my dragon's
tiny head rose from under the covers. He scanned the
room frantically for a few seconds but when he saw me

he scurried across the floor and leapt onto my shoulder. I loved having Ketchup around. Just the thought of him being vacuumed up made me shiver. But we were safe. For now…

I didn't go up into my room much the next day. You might think it was mean to leave Ketchup on his own but it was to stop attracting suspicion. When it was finally 8 o'clock I felt it was late enough and went up to my room. After checking no one else was in there I said "Come on, you're safe?" Ketchup staggered out from behind the wardrobe, utterly terrified. "What's wrong?" I asked, and walked closer to the wardrobe. That's when I saw it, shining in the moonlight. A dart.

CHAPTER 5

I stood there, frozen, staring at the thing on the floor.
I felt…scared. My dragon had become part of my
life now, was I going to lose him? I stood dazed for
a moment, with my mouth gaping open until I was
snapped out of it by Ketchup whimpering. I was
breathing heavily, my heart thumping in my chest. I
took the dart and put it on my bedside table.

I barely got any sleep that night and not even the
warmth and soft light under the covers was enough
to stop me thinking of losing Ketchup. I found a new
hiding spot for Ketchup, under my bed is a big clump
of old soft toys, he blends in perfectly so it's the ideal

hiding spot. Even Ketchup likes it, and trust me, getting him to like something is not easy! So Ketchup should be safe for now. I had even managed to cram the toys together so you couldn't see him from any angle... then I realised something - Ketchup had been hiding in the wardrobe with some fries since the morning, which means... "Oh no" I whispered.

I immediately felt scared. "How could I have done this?" I thought. I felt so stupid. I didn't guard the one piece of evidence, besides Ketchup of course. I'd been so worried about hiding my dragon that I had forgotten. I then felt a small pat on my shoulder, it was Ketchup, perched on my shoulder. I tried to smile but I couldn't. I felt so bad for him, not knowing how careless I had been. But then I sighed and thought better not to dwell on it. That night I treasured sleeping with my dragon more than ever before.

I know I said you could trust her with anything but I didn't tell Olive what Dad had found. So I guess I'm the only one who knows, back to being drained by my secret. But I knew it was for the best. I decided to talk to Dad just to see if he really had it. I knew it was risky but I was prepared to take that chance. I had to find out either way, good or bad.

But I never got the chance to ask him, with his work and my homework, I could never find the right time; until finally one evening I cornered him on the landing. He turned to face me and sighed. "I wasn't sure you were ready for this…" he said, pulling out the photo print, the one I had taken.

I felt a flood of shock and fear flow through me, even though I knew he must have the photo it was still a surprise to see it in Dad's hand.

CHAPTER 6

"*This*," said Dad, "is living in our house."

He showed the photograph and I screamed with pretend shock, looking at the photo with wide eyes. Dad put a comforting hand on my shoulder and said "Don't worry, I won't stop until," his chest swollen with pride, "I hunt down that vile creature and save us all." Something inside me just snapped, BOOM. I tried to stop myself but I couldn't. I shouted at him "He is not vile!" Dad took a step towards me, "What did you say?" he asked.

"Ermmm…Err…" I spluttered, "He's not vile, he's… disgusting! Disgustingly vile!"

I felt horrible, I wanted to run to my room and hide under the covers until he was gone but instead I stood there as Dad smiled at me and said "That's the spirit!" He then walked downstairs leaving me with my thoughts. That moment I spotted Ketchup, perched on my bedroom door handle. He had orange tears running down his little face. That night he wouldn't sleep next to me. "What have I done?" I thought to myself.

When I was younger, I thought Dad's job meant he caught mythical creatures; but this had gotten out of hand. Ketchup didn't eat the fries I gave him the next day but he warmed up to me a little. After a few days though it was back to normal. "You're not vile," I said as I got dressed for school, "You're amazing." I saw my dragon's scales shimmer when he heard that. So now I had sorted out Ketchup but I have no idea how I'm going to sort out Dad…

I decided to try and stick Ketchup's wings down so he looked like a normal lizard. I still didn't know if this would stop Dad trying to catch him though. I thought I would still give it a go, but when I did Ketchup shot out of my hands and started flying around my room! Yes! FLYING! It was incredible. He twisted and turned effortlessly and when he landed on the ground he had that smug look on his face again. I grinned when I realised he was obviously very proud of himself.

I told Olive at school the next day and she loved it! "Whoa! So cool!" she exclaimed. When I then told Ketchup about Olive's reaction he looked more smug than ever. It made me think what it would be like to be a dragon. To be able to fly, to breathe fire (or at least sparks like Ketchup) and to be free and happy. It must feel epic. But then I realised something, Ketchup wasn't free. So I started to form a plan. A plan… to release Ketchup.

I didn't want to think of releasing Ketchup as that meant I would lose my dragon pet. I tried to think of a way I could keep him but whether I liked it or not releasing him was for the better. I told Olive of my plan and she almost cried. But I couldn't concentrate on Olive right now. I needed to get home. I wasn't releasing Ketchup just yet but I needed to tell him. He often seemed to know what I was saying. I felt sad knowing that no longer having Ketchup was my own idea. I wondered how I'd feel, apart from sad of course. But I continued forming the plan and eventually I had a blueprint. Everything was planned out. Now I just need to work out when to do it…

I decided to do it on my birthday, when everyone else would be distracted.

So I had a plan and a date set but goodness knows what might happen between now and then. So I had to keep Ketchup hidden as much as possible.

At school I laid out my plan for Ketchup's release to Olive. It was pretty much foolproof. When I'd finished she squealed with delight. "Why so happy?" I asked. "I have something," she said, her eyes shining. "Come over on Friday," she whispered. "You're going to love it."

I checked with Mum and she was fine with me going over to Olive's. So now I could go but what was this big 'surprise'? I don't really like surprises, waiting for this really good thing for ages before finally you get it and discover that maybe it's not that great after all. But it was Monday of all days, so I still had 4 days to wait before finding out what this surprise was going to be, hopefully it was worth the wait... I wanted to know now but when I asked Olive she just smiled and said

"I'll show you Friday". Nothing much happened the next few days, Tuesday was boring, Wednesday was boring, Thursday was slightly less boring until finally Friday arrived. The big day. I couldn't wait for home time. When my mum dropped me off I could wait no longer, "Come up here!" I heard Olive shout from upstairs. I raced up at full speed. I walked into Olive's room… and there, sitting on her bed, was a small, yellow dragon.

CHAPTER 7

It looked up when it saw me and flew around my head, sniffing me, before resting on Olive's lap. Olive had the biggest smile on her face. "She's called Amber!" she blurted out. Amber's scales were glossy and her wings much longer than Ketchup's. She showed off doing somersaults, flips and even a dive in the air; which didn't go too well, to say the least. She crash-landed onto the bed and when her face appeared from under the covers I could see her cheeks go red. She was still elegant in the air, although Olive told me she didn't shoot sparks. Olive and I talked about dragons and played with Amber until it was time for me to go home. Now, I know I said I hate surprises, but that one was definitely worth the wait.

I told Ketchup about it that night and he huffed when I told him about Amber. It was like he was saying "There's no dragon better than me." I smiled and scooped him up, before perching him on my bed. He scrambled under the covers, almost beckoning me to join him. As usual, I enjoyed a nice warm sleep with Ketchup.

I had a spring in my step the next morning: Saturday - perfect. I told Mum Olive had a new video game so I could go to her house again, only I would be bringing Ketchup this time. But Mum had been getting really suspicious after my secretive behaviour since finding Ketchup, so she eyed me and simply said "No, not today." I had an experiment in mind but it looked like that was going to have to wait for now. I knew Dad hadn't seen Ketchup because he was safe under my bed, but it was only a matter of time before he found him; so I had to be prepared for when he did. I improved Ketchup's hiding spot so that he was practically invisible. I also made it harder to move the toys and if you tried, it would hit a squeaky toy, alerting Ketchup. It was like a full on base. An impenetrable base.

I didn't manage to see Amber again. Compared to Amber, Ketchup's wings were tiny. No wonder she started flying so early. She's like an air acrobat. I couldn't wait to see her again. This must be how Olive felt about Ketchup.

On Monday I went to get Ketchup after school. I looked under my bed and sure enough the big clump of toys was still there. "Ketchup?" I called. Nothing. "Ketchup!" I called again. Still nothing. I moved the clump of toys, setting off the squeaky toy and Ketchup wasn't there.

CHAPTER 8

No no no NO! Where was he? I panicked, how could
I have lost him? Was he still hiding? Then I suddenly
thought - what if Dad had got him? I rushed to Olive's
and told her everything. There was a pause- an awkward
one - before Olive tried to calm me by saying she was
sure Ketchup could hold on until we could find a way
to rescue him.

I had a sleepless night until the next morning when I
was walking to school with Olive and I heard the noisy
engine of the pest control van. As it drove past I could
see in one of the cages, Ketchup. He stared at me with
sad little eyes. It was only a moment we looked into
each other's eyes, but it felt like hours. I was blown

back by the rush of air from the van, knocked back into reality. And I knew there was nothing that was going to stand in my way of getting him back.

I told Olive to go get Amber, I had a plan. But we didn't have much time… 10 minutes later, Olive was back holding Amber. I rushed to my house with Olive following close behind. Mum was surprised when we both turned up at the door, "What the?!" she spluttered, jumping when she caught sight of Amber. And I don't exactly blame her… "It's okay," I said. "She's friendly." Olive added. Amber fluttered around Mum before perching on her head. I could see Mum calm a little, and she held out her hand. Amber flew on to it, she looked at Mum with a warm smile. I explained everything to Mum, about Dad and Ketchup.

When I finished, Mum had a determined look in her eyes as she announced "Let's do this!" We ran to her car and moments later we were on the road. I sat in the front with Olive behind me playing with Amber.

It made me miss Ketchup… It felt like an eternity until we finally pulled up at the pest control centre. Mum stayed to park the car and Olive and I climbed out of the car and entered the building. There were lots of nets hanging up, and wild animals in cages on the floor. An evil-looking rat glared at us through a tight metal cage. Olive suggested we split up, I took Amber and Olive set off to find Ketchup. Amber and I went through a door and walked down a corridor. As we turned the corner we ran straight into Dad.

"Wha…?" he began, before his confusion turned to anger when he spotted Amber. When he took out his dart gun and started loading it, the tiny dragon let out a whimper. "Wait!" I cried. Dad lowered the gun, his initial confusion returning. "Look at her," I said. It was time to explain everything to Dad. "She won't harm you, and neither will my dragon. Not unless he's provoked." Dad chuckled. Behind me, Ketchup snarled. At this Amber started to snarl too. His face soured.

You see, Dad hadn't noticed - while he was busy loading his dart gun - that Olive had returned with Ketchup, she had found him! We all closed in on Dad. But then suddenly the gun fired, and a dart missed Ketchup by a hair's width. In that moment, all my confidence vanished. There was nothing we could do now. But then Amber let out an almighty roar. It blew Dad's hair back, it was so fierce. Amber's previously orange eyes turned a fiery red. She bit Dad on the leg and he dropped his gun. I kicked it out of reach with my foot as Dad muttered "Why this little..." through gritted teeth. Amber seemed to have returned to normal. "Wow!" I thought. That certainly made up for no fire! Dad whispered, "I give up. You win," as he grasped his injured leg. I helped him up and we all drove back home in silence. I felt worried about him. Even after all he'd done, was this really right? I slunk back in my seat, ashamed.

My worry soon vanished though when I heard it wasn't a serious bite and that he would soon heal.

After all the drama, I had almost forgotten my experiment. Ketchup is a boy dragon and Amber is a girl dragon, so maybe… Well you can guess the rest. Anyway, Mum was fine with it as she's friendly with the dragons now. But she still sounded a bit nervous and I could see she was still worried about Dad. When I got to Olive's she was excited to see how the experiment would go. We put the two dragons on the bedroom floor and waited…

Ketchup circled Amber, sniffing her. Amber just sat there and didn't really move much. Then Ketchup stopped circling and nuzzled Amber. She then nuzzled him back. They smiled, and shot into the air. They each fired a spark into the air, and they struck, showering us with tiny flickers. They made a few acrobatic moves after that, then rested back onto the bed. Olive and I just sat in awe, before blinking and sneezing. It was really hard to get Ketchup to leave after that; but it took a lot for me to leave too.

CHAPTER 9

When Dad was fully healed he started to warm up
to the dragons a bit. Ketchup helped Mum and Dad,
by calming them after a long day of work. His magic
worked on them too; his light and warmth was like an
endless spa. By this point Olive's family liked dragons
too. Life was just better with Ketchup around. But then
I remembered - I had to release him eventually. My
birthday was edging closer…

Most kids would be happy it was nearly their birthday
but not me. Releasing my awesome new(ish) pet didn't
seem that great to me Anyway, I figured it was best to
make the most of it while it lasted so I tried to do that.
Then Olive told me how she found Amber but (no
offence Olive) it was really really long and really really

boring so in a nutshell, here is how Olive found Amber: "We had set up a nature camera in our garden and we were constantly getting these weird scaly feet crawling across the patio. So we decided to investigate. We had searched for weeks and my parents had given up; after all, we weren't seeing the feet any more. Until one day, I was outside in my garden when I heard a strange noise coming from our new hedgehog house. Hedgehogs! I thought, but oh no…Inside was some kind of mutant lizard."

That was Amber of course. But it was very interesting. To be honest, much more interesting than my story of how I found Ketchup. Thinking back to that first night, it was kind of absurd that I'd found him in a wardrobe, chewing cloth… I mean, come on, does that really sound dramatic to you? (I still hadn't been found out for reading at night!) Although it is pretty absurd finding a dragon anyway…

It was the evening of my birthday. Everyone was

distracted downstairs but Mum, Dad, Olive and Amber were up in my bedroom with me. We all said our goodbyes before Mum opened the window. I took a deep breath. Olive did too. "Goodbye Ketchup," I said. "Goodbye Amber," said Olive. We all watched as they fluttered into the stars, doing a few twists and turns, before disappearing into the night sky.

And I got a lot of great presents on my birthday: but Ketchup's freedom was the greatest gift of all.

3 WEEKS LATER

I was clearing out all of Ketchup's old stuff to put in a safe place. The ragged clothes, the chewed up fries - every one was a precious memory. That was when I noticed them. It only took a moment to realise what they were…

DRAGON EGGS!!!

Continue the story in "There's a Dragon in My Wardrobe: Mayhem with a Capital M!"...

Printed in Great Britain
by Amazon

21288087R00038